The Manzanar Scrapbook

PRAISE FOR *STORYSHARES*

"One of the brightest innovators and game-changers in the education industry."
– Forbes

"Your success in applying research-validated practices to promote literacy serves as a valuable model for other organizations seeking to create evidence-based literacy programs."
- Library of Congress

"We need powerful social and educational innovation, and Storyshares is breaking new ground. The organization addresses critical problems facing our students and teachers. I am excited about the strategies it brings to the collective work of making sure every student has an equal chance in life."
– Teach For America

"Around the world, this is one of the up-and-coming trailblazers changing the landscape of literacy and education."
- International Literacy Association

"It's the perfect idea. There's really nothing like this. I mean wow, this will be a wonderful experience for young people."   - Andrea Davis Pinkney, Executive Director, Scholastic

"Reading for meaning opens opportunities for a lifetime of learning. Providing emerging readers with engaging texts that are designed to offer both challenges and support for each individual will improve their lives for years to come. Storyshares is a wonderful start."
- David Rose, Co-founder of CAST & UDL

The Manzanar Scrapbook

Brian Kirchner

STORYSHARES

Story Share, Inc.
New York. Boston. Philadelphia

Published in the United States by Story Share, Inc.

The characters and events in this book are fictitious. Any similarity to real persons, living or dead, is entirely coincidental.

Storyshares
Story Share, Inc.
24 N. Bryn Mawr Avenue #340
Bryn Mawr, PA 19010-3304
www.storyshares.org

Inspiring reading with a new kind of book.

Interest Level: High School
Grade Level Equivalent: 3.8

9781973471288

Book design by Storyshares

Printed in the United States of America

Storyshares Presents

1

As soon as I stepped outside, my nose and ears got numb. In about ten more seconds, the rest of my face was frozen, too.

It was early December 2017, and Michigan was having the harshest cold snap in years, according to all of the TV weather people. Right now, at 7:10 PM in my town of Redford, the temperature was a brisk 10 degrees. Below zero, that is.

And that didn't count the wind chill factor.

I rolled my wool ski cap down over my ears and tried to use my big, insulated mittens to warm my face. It didn't work. I resigned myself to turning into an icicle during the short walk to band practice. I wondered briefly how long it would take, once I got there, to warm my hands up enough to be able to play my guitar. Twenty minutes minimum, judging by how cold they were already getting, even with the warm mittens on.

My band, by the way, is called the People Movers. We're named after the world's lamest mass transit system. It's an elevated rail in Detroit that goes in a loop around the central downtown business and sports district. It stops at the Renaissance Center, Cobo Hall, Joe Louis Arena, and a few other places, and that's about it. It's great if you're a tourist and want to see the amazing sights of the Motor City (yes, sarcasm definitely intended here), but if you're a regular Joe or Jill who needs it to actually get places, it's pretty useless.

Even so, my buddies and I thought it would be a good name for our band, which is kind of a fusion of rock and funk. In other words, we play music that moves people. Thus, People Movers.

It was only three blocks from my house to our bass player's, but it felt like twenty. There was a nasty wind blowing against me the whole way. By the time I got there I was trying to remember if face transplants were a thing yet. I hoped so.

I knocked on the front door, and after a minute our bassist's grandfather answered. He smiled at me and bowed a little bit, then let me in.

Let me explain the bowing thing. Our bassist is Kenji Omura. He was born in Detroit, and his grandparents were born in California, but his great-grandparents both came here from Japan before the First World War. Kenji's grandpa, whose name is Franklin, still had some of the Japanese traditions that his folks handed down, like bowing. I thought it was pretty cool, although it took me awhile to get used to bowing back. But now I did it without even thinking.

Mr. Omura is a little guy, not even as tall as me and I'm only five-six. He was wearing baggy green corduroys, a red and green checked shirt, and bright rainbow suspenders a la Mork from Ork. His black hair stuck out in all directions like he'd just been wrestling with the Omura's golden retriever, Honey. Which he probably had been.

"Hey, Carlos!" he said, closing the front door. "Band practice night again already?"

"Yep," I said, stepping into the living room and taking off my coat, hat, and mittens. "Every Tuesday, Mr. Omura."

Kenji's mom and dad were sitting together in the living room, watching something on the DIY channel.

"Carlos!" said his dad. His name was Junichi but everyone called him John. "How's everything in your neck of the woods?"

"Great, thanks, Mr. Omura," I said. "Hi, Mrs. Omura."

"Hi there, Carlos, nice to see you,"
Jillian Omura replied, smiling at me. Kenji's folks were awesome people. Very cool.

Kenji's grandpa said, "Hey, you guys are sounding good! What's that one you always play, the Jimi Hendrix one..."

"Crosstown Traffic?" I said.

He snapped his bony fingers. "Yeah, that's it. Sounds awesome, really groovy!" He started snapping fingers on both hands and doing a little shuck-and-jive.

The dude cracked me up.

"Thanks," I said. "Our new drummer really pulled us together."

"Yusuf? He's the bomb! He can really bang the skins, baby!" He played some furious air drums.

The dude really cracked me up.

Just then, the doorbell rang. Franklin opened it. On the porch was a pizza delivery guy, holding a steaming cardboard box. I could smell it from inside the house.

"Pizza's here!" yelled Franklin. To the pizza guy he said, "Come on in and warm up, man." He opened the door and the guy stepped in. His nametag read, "Hi, I'm BRAD!"

"Thanks," said Brad, shivering. "Freezing out there."

Before Franklin could respond, a furious barking shattered the air. The Omura's golden retriever, Honey, came charging out of the kitchen and barreled straight for

Brad. She was like a yellow blur. Brad shrieked and jumped backwards. The pizza almost fell out of his hands, but Franklin grabbed it in the nick of time.

"Honey! Down!" Franklin yelled, grabbing Honey's leather collar with one hand while balancing the pizza with the other. It was quite a sight, and I gave the old man props for his agility. "Down! Stop it!"

The sound of Franklin's voice calmed the dog down, but she still eyed Brad warily. Brad returned the favor times ten. He clearly wasn't convinced that he wasn't going to get mauled.

"That's a high-strung dog you got there," said Brad.

"Aw, she's okay," said Franklin with a big grin. "She's really mellow, actually. She only gets that way around strangers."

"Oh. All right." Brad didn't sound reassured.

Kenji came into the living room from the kitchen.

"Hey, Carlos," he said. "Lemme pay for this and we can go down and jam." He pulled some bills out of his pocket and handed them over to Brad. "Keep the change.

Consider it compensation for having to deal with our unhinged dog."

"Cool, thanks," said Brad, stuffing the cash in his front pocket without counting it and bolting out the door.

Franklin closed it behind him. A gust of frigid air swept past me.

"You guys oughta have a cowbell on that dog or something," I said.

Franklin busted out laughing as he handed the pizza over to Kenji. "Yeah, cowbell! Nice! More cowbell!"

"Yeah, all right, okay, Grandpa. Carlos and I have band practice, you know?"

"Sure," Franklin said. "Hey, Carlos, I want you to meet someone before you head down."

Kenji rolled his eyes. "Grandpa, not Mr. Tanaka," he said with a sigh.

"It'll just take a sec," Franklin replied. "Scout's honor." He held up three fingers in the Boy Scout salute.

"You weren't ever a Boy Scout," said Kenji.

"So what? Come on, Carlos, I promise, just for a minute." He grabbed me by the wrist and started pulling me with him.

"Okay," I said. "But just for a minute."

"Yeah, no problem. Come on."

2

Franklin led me through the living room to the back of the house. We went into a spare bedroom that had been converted into a little man cave for Kenji's grandpa. There was an old, brown leather sofa and a couple of La-Z-Boy recliners, along with the prerequisite big-screen TV and beer fridge.

Sitting on the sofa was a man who looked like he was probably about Franklin Omura's age, mid-eighties or so. He looked like he'd be really tall if he stood up; his knees were practically touching his chest. He wore an old UCLA sweatshirt and blue jeans, and his hair, which was practically white, was combed back from his forehead like the Fonz on Happy Days. He was holding a Pabst Blue Ribbon.

"Carlos, meet Hideki Tanaka, my old buddy!" said Franklin.

Mr. Tanaka stood up, and I was right: the guy was at least six-foot-three. His grin widened, and he extended a long, bony hand. I shook it.

"Hideki and I go way back," said Franklin. "All the way back to the war. We were kids out in California together."

Mr. Tanaka clapped Franklin on the back. "Oh, yeah. The good old days, right, Frankie?"

"You got that right. Carlos, I gotta tell you about what this old dog and I did back in nineteen fifty-two—"

"Hey, I'm really sorry, Mr. Omura, but the other guys are waiting on me, you know what I mean?"

"Oh, yeah, no problem," Franklin said.

"Go do your thing, Carlos," said Mr. Tanaka. "Frankie's told me all about the People Movers. Rock on!"

Then the guy actually flashed me the forked heavy metal sign. Was this the twenty-first century or the nineteen-eighties?

"Uh, yeah, right on. Pleasure to meet you, Mr. Tanaka." I backed out and closed the door.

In the basement, everyone was already set up. There was Kenji tuning up his Fender Jazz bass; Yusuf working out some new beats on the drum kit and wearing his trademark straw cowboy hat, which had a hole in it from an incident the previous summer involving Derek Bodley, the local knucklehead; and, of course, our lead singer, Xavier Montgomery Maplethorpe, whom everyone just called X. He was fifteen, the same age as the rest of us, but was six feet tall and thin as a rail. His head was covered by a fluffy afro the size of a beach ball that bobbed gently whenever he moved his head.

X was the man: he had a voice like Jimi Hendrix, moves like James Brown, and a brain like Sherlock Holmes. Last summer, he'd gotten Yusuf off the hook when old Derek Bodley had tried to frame Yusuf for some skanky graffiti sprayed on the Bodley garage. It was a real close call, too. With the Make America Safe Again laws, Yusuf's family, who were Syrian refugees, nearly got deported before X was able to prove Bodley himself had done the deed. Real class act, that Bodley. But Yusuf and his family were safe now, living in a little apartment in the neighborhood, and believe me when I tell you my man Yusuf could make those skins rock and roll like nobody I'd ever seen.

There were high fives all around when I came in. My Fender Strat was where I'd left it after the last practice, leaning in one corner, and I started setting up.

"Yo, Carlos!" said X into his mic, his voice booming out through his amp. "How you be, my brother?"

"Just kickin' it, you know," I answered, putting my guitar on and plugging in. I struck a power G chord, relishing the solid, crunching tone. I looked at Kenji, who was still fiddling with his bass's tuning keys. "Dude, your grandpa is something else, man."

Kenji rolled his eyes. "Don't remind me, Carlos. He just gets weirder every year."

"Aw, cut your gramps some slack!" said X. "He's himself, that's all. Most folks don't have the guts to really be who they are inside. I give him big props."

Yusuf nodded from behind his kit. "Mr. Omura is awesome! I like him very much."

Yusuf's English had improved since we'd met him last summer, and he only occasionally found himself searching for the right word. He'd also taught us a little Arabic. Mostly swear words, naturally.

"Yeah, well, try living with the guy," said Kenji. "It's not so awesome. Last Saturday, he was outside shoveling snow and singing some old song from the forties at the top of his lungs. And dancing, for God's sake. Dancing with his snow shovel! People were staring."

"Dancin' with his shovel?" hooted X.
"Franklin Omura, the man, the legend! Right on! What was he singing?"

"The same thing he always sings, man," said Kenji. "That one he learned when he was a kid in the camp. The Frank Sinatra one. So lame."

"Oh yeah," I said. "'New York, New York'. I like that one, actually. For a tune that the T-rexes probably grooved to back in the day, it's not bad."

"Yeah, that's the one," said Kenji.

"Camp?" said Yusuf. "Like, summer camp?"

Kenji shook his head. "Nope. Not like summer camp at all. Internment camp. During World War Two."

"What's internment?" said Yusuf.

"Like a concentration camp," X said. "Bad mojo." He shook his head. His Afro waved in the air. "Most definitely not cool."

Yusuf said, "Your grandfather was in a concentration camp, Kenji? But I thought only Nazis had them."

"The Nazis had the really bad ones," said Kenji. "But America had some, too. Anyone Japanese living on the West Coast got put into them until the war was over. Even if you were an American citizen, they put you in there. Didn't matter who you were or if you ever did anything wrong. If you were Japanese or Japanese-American, you had to go."

Yusuf looked a little shocked. "But... in America? I've been in refugee camps and they were bad. It's hard to imagine something like this in America."

Kenji nodded. "Yeah. But it happened. Check it out on Wikipedia. Just don't ask my grandpa, he doesn't like to talk about it." He paused, like he wasn't sure whether to say more. Then he continued. "He was only twelve or so when his family got thrown in one of the camps they had in California. Out in the desert, a total wasteland. His mom and sister died there. He told me about it when I was little, after he'd had a little too much to drink one night."

X whistled. "Heavy, bro."

"Yeah," said Kenji. "I don't know how they died. Grandpa didn't want to tell me. And none of you guys should ask him about it."

"Of course not," said Yusuf. "We would never show him such disrespect."

"He introduced me to his friend, Mr. Tanaka, when I got here," I said.

"Yeah, Mr. Tanaka's a character," Kenji said, smiling. "Funny guy. I guess he and Grandpa met in the camp, actually."

"Seems like a cool guy," I said.

"Yeah, he's the bomb. He sold my folks a safe last month. He runs a locksmith shop. The safe is top of the line, but he gave them a huge discount on it."

"Why did they need a safe?" asked Yusuf.

"Dad got Mom this sweet necklace for her birthday last month, and they needed a place to keep it. I told them they should get a safe deposit box at the bank, but Mom wanted the necklace close by so she could look at it whenever she wants. It's got all these diamonds, and there's a couple of bright blue stones, too…"

"Sapphires?" I asked.

Kenji nodded. "Yeah, sapphires. This thing must have cost a fortune, you guys. Seriously." He thought for a moment. "Hey, you guys want to see it? I bet Mom would show it to you."

Yusuf and I were down with this idea. X looked impatient to start practice but went along with it. We all followed Kenji upstairs. His mom and dad were still watching TV, but Jillian Omura readily agreed to show us the necklace. I don't think she needed much of an excuse to show it off.

3

The safe was upstairs in the master bedroom. It was a solid-looking black metal cube standing on four legs that lifted it about three inches off the gray, deep-pile carpet. On the door was an electronic display window and a keypad, a chrome handle, and a logo that showed an eagle with a big key clutched in its talons with the words "Sentry Safe" written across it in silver block letters.

"Electronic lock," X commented. "Good choice, Mrs. O. Almost impossible to break into."

"Well, Hideki Tanaka really recommended it," she replied, then knelt down and entered a code into the keypad, which emitted a series of loud electronic boops and beeps. "This thing makes a racket, doesn't it?" she said.

Then she grasped the handle, turned it, and the safe swung open. She reached in and withdrew a small jewelry box made of lacquered black wood. She lifted the lid.

Inside, resting in a little nest of black velvet, was the most amazing necklace I'd ever seen outside of a museum. It was just like Kenji had described it: it was a pendant set with two large sapphires and several smaller diamonds. The sapphires were a deep blue color that seemed to go on forever, and the diamonds sparked off tiny rainbows of light. The whole thing was attached to a thin gold chain.

"Whoa," I breathed. "Rockin'."

"That's beautiful, Mrs. Omura!" exclaimed Yusuf, his eyes wide. His straw cowboy hat was teetering on his head, threatening to fall off. He didn't seem to notice. "Amazing!"

Mrs. Omura smiled again, wider this time. "Thank you, Carlos and Yusuf."

"Are you ever going to wear it, Mom?" asked Kenji.

"I wore it that one time when your father took me out to dinner for my birthday last month," she replied, stroking the necklace with one fingertip. "I don't know if I have the nerve to do it again! The whole time I felt like I was wearing our life savings around my neck."

"How much did this thing cost, anyway?" said Kenji.

"Your dad still won't tell me," she said with a laugh. "He said he'd been socking away his work bonuses for a year and didn't spend any family money on it." She rolled her eyes. "John is such a romantic. I guess he wants it to be a mystery."

"Mrs. O, this necklace really is the bomb," said X, who had been standing near the bedroom doorway and looking restless. "But, fellas, can we get down to business? We got some jams to practice, brothers."

"Right on, X," I said. "Hey, Mrs. Omura, thanks for showing this to us. It's really cool."

"You're welcome, Carlos." She grinned and put her finger to her lips. "But don't tell anyone. Mum's the word!"

We all laughed. Then Kenji spoke up.

"What's that, Mom?" he asked, pointing inside the safe. There was a small book sitting in there. It had an orange plastic cover.

"Oh, that's your grandfather's," said Mrs. Omura. "It's an old scrapbook of some kind. He asked us to keep it in here for him. It's very private, he asked us not to look at it. But it must be pretty important to him."

"That's awesome, super-fine, for sure," said X. He was getting so impatient I thought sparks might start shooting out of his big Afro. "Can we practice now?"

4

"Guys, my house got busted into!"

This came from Kenji. He was out of breath after running all the way from his place to mine. It was Sunday afternoon, and he'd texted X, Yusuf, and me to meet him here.

"Say what?" exclaimed X.

"Yeah, sometime since our last practice on Tuesday," said Kenji, stripping off his parka and ski hat. He began pacing around my living room and running one hand through his thick mop of black hair. "This is messed up, you guys. Messed. Up."

"Was anything stolen?" Yusuf asked.

"That's the weirdest part," said Kenji. "My mom's necklace and Grandpa's book got ripped off from that safe in my parents' bedroom. But... the safe door was still locked. Mom opened it yesterday evening. She was going to get her necklace because she and Dad were going to see the symphony last night. She opened the safe and — empty! Poof! Everything gone." He made a gesture with his hands like a small explosion.

"Hold up," said X. "You're tellin' us the goods just disappeared? The safe wasn't cracked or anything?"

"Well, it must have been cracked somehow," said Kenji. "How else would anyone get into it? You guys all saw it. Electronic lock, supposed to be unbreakable? Ha! That's a crock." He ran his hand distractedly through his hair again. "This is scary, man! Some stranger was in my house! We could've all gotten killed or kidnapped or something."

"Yeah, but you didn't, so don't go getting all worked up about that," said X. "How'd this jive turkey thief get into your house in the first place?"

"He got in through the back, the sliding glass door onto the patio. It was unlocked. He just slid it open and walked right in, man!"

I knew Kenji needed to chill, so I went to the kitchen and grabbed a cold Coke from the fridge. I went back to the living room.

"Yo, heads up," I said, and tossed him the can. He snagged it with one hand.

"Thanks," he said. He popped the top and took a long swig. "Okay. All right. I needed that."

"So your folks didn't give you any more 411?" said X.

"No, they don't know much. The cops just finished going over the house a couple hours ago. I guess they'll tell my parents if they find anything."

"How is your grandfather?" asked Yusuf.

Kenji frowned. "Yeah, Grandpa. That's the weirdest part. He's way more upset than me or my folks. Guys, he was crying when he found out. I've never seen him cry before."

"Hard to imagine," I said. "He's always being goofy. Seems like a really happy dude. Any idea why he's so freaked out?"

"It's because his little book got stolen." Kenji shook his head. "I don't know, fellas. Never seen the old guy like this before. Just sitting at the kitchen table with his head down, sobbing. Like he lost a relative or something."

X, who had been lounging in a big bowl-shaped wicker chair in one corner, suddenly jumped up, unfolding his six-foot frame and making his fro bob and weave. "My brothers, let's jet over to my place and talk to my pops. Maybe he knows something about this. There's something going on here. I have a funky feeling, and not the good kind."

5

"Well, I don't know too much," said Monty Maplethorpe in his bullfrog voice. "But my buddy Rintz gave me a heads-up about an hour ago 'cause he knows you boys are friends with the Omuras. He got a little info from the guy in charge of the case."

Detective Montgomery Maplethorpe was sitting in his favorite easy chair in the living room at X's house and, as usual, smoking a big cigar. The cracked red leather squeaked and groaned under his weight as he shifted his bad leg to a more comfortable position. X's dad was semi-retired from the Redford Police Department, where he'd been a cop for the last eighteen years before being injured on the job.

The living room walls were covered with framed commendations and photos of him with the mayor, the police chief, and a bunch of other bigwigs. Detective Maplethorpe knew practically everyone in the Redford P.D., and sometimes he gave X the lowdown on neighborhood malfeasance.

"For real?" said X. "Lay it on us, Pops."

We were all gathered around the detective, sitting on kitchen chairs dragged in for the powwow. A cloud of foul-smelling smoke drifted past us from his cigar. I tried to take shallow breaths, imagining the crud that smoke contained.

"First off, no fingerprints anywhere. No surprise there. Whoever it was probably wore gloves. No other trace evidence, nothing to pull a DNA sample from. Very careful work, I gotta say."

Kenji looked disappointed. "Anything else?"

"Yeah, one thing. Doesn't look like anything in the house was disturbed except for the safe. No signs of a search, no drawers opened, nothing like that. Usually when there's a home break-in, we can find something that indicates the perpetrator looked around the place for a while. Not this time."

"So they headed right for the safe," said X.

Monty nodded. "Looks that way right now, anyway. Might not mean anything. The master bedroom's a natural target for a burglar, since that's usually where the jewelry is."

"But the safe..." I said.

"Yeah," he said, nodding. "How'd the perpetrator get into the safe? Good question. Electronic lock, a high-end one."

"We saw it," said Yusuf.

"And the safe door was closed and locked when Kenji's mom discovered the necklace was missing. So either the guy picked an electronic lock, or the goods just evaporated into thin air."

"There's no way the burglar picked that lock, Pops," said X. "Uh-uh."

"It would've been a tricky job, but the guy did it. Somehow. Must have."

"Nope," said X. "I ain't saying it would've been hard to do. I ain't saying I don't think he picked it. I'm sayin' I know he didn't."

Monty Maplethorpe squinted at his tall, gangly son through the cloud of cigar smoke. "What're you trying to say, Xavier?"

"Fellas," X said, looking at me and Kenji and Yusuf. "Remember how much noise that keypad made when Mrs. O opened it to show us the necklace?"

"Yeah," said Yusuf, nodding. His big straw cowboy hat, as always, miraculously remained perched on his head. "Loud."

"Right on. You guys think Kenji's folks would've slept through that kind of noise? You can't break an electronic lock without using the keypad. And that keypad would've woken up anyone within fifty feet."

"Maybe it happened during the day, when everyone was gone," said Yusuf.

X shook his head, making his Afro jiggle. "Nope, my brother. The dog. Remember how Honey freaked out when the pizza guy came into the house?"

"Right," said Kenji. "That dog goes ballistic when strangers come in."

"So there's no way the burglar could've got past Honey," I said. "But wouldn't that be true if the break-in happened at night, too? The burglar wouldn't have gotten more than five steps into the house no matter what time of day it was, as long as Honey was around."

"Honey's been sleeping in the basement for the last few weeks," said Kenji. "She wakes up at night sometimes, and if she's in someone's bed she'll want to play. We weren't getting any sleep."

"Okay, then," said X. "This must have gone down at night while Honey was sleeping downstairs. The guy gets into the house through the patio door, goes up to the safe, and... then what? He didn't pick the lock, would've been too loud. But he got the thing open somehow."

Kenji spoke up. "This all seems like a stretch, you guys. The burglar just happens to be an expert safecracker and just happens to pick a house with a high-end safe containing a jewelry jackpot?"

"What's a safecracker?" asked Yusuf. "How do you crack a safe?" He looked genuinely puzzled.

"It's someone who breaks into safes for a living," Kenji said, smiling for the first time that day. "They don't literally crack it, though. They pick the lock. Safecracker is a figure of speech."

Yusuf nodded. "I get it. English is strange. Too many figures of speech."

"What about Arabic, dude?" I said. "Don't forget all the stuff we've learned from you. Stuff like—"

Yusuf cut me off. "Please, no, Carlos, not here. Whatever you were about to say, don't say it."

"Fine, okay." Not that Detective Maplethorpe would have understood me, but I'd been about to spout some pretty juicy Arabic gutter talk Yusuf had taught us back during the summer. I decided to save it for later.

"Yeah, right, anyway," said X impatiently. "So either we got a major coincidence, or the guy who broke in knew what he was after." He thought for a moment. "Hey,

Kenji, your mom ever wear that necklace out on the town? She tell people about it?"

Kenji shook his head. "Not really. She wore it out to dinner on her birthday, but I think that's it. It's been in the safe ever since, as far as I know. And I don't know for sure how many people she's told about it. Probably not too many. She isn't the bragging type. I'm guessing she didn't spread the word around much."

"Right on, right on," said X. "So the people who knew about the necklace for sure are your folks, you, and your grandpa. A few people saw it when your mom and dad were out for the birthday dinner. And she probably hasn't told anyone. That about right?"

Kenji nodded. "Yeah, I think so." He frowned. "Wait. There is one more person."

"Who's that?" I asked.

"Hideki Tanaka."

"Hid achey tonna who?" said Detective Maplethorpe.

"Naw, pops, Hideki Tanaka!" said X. "It ain't that hard to pronounce."

X's dad frowned, but remained silent.

"Old guy, friend of Grandpa's," Kenji continued. "He comes by the house sometimes. He and Grandpa play cards and have a few beers together. They talk about the war sometimes, too. Mr. Tanaka's the only one Grandpa will talk about the war with. I'm pretty sure Grandpa told him about the necklace. Grandpa's proud that my dad is successful enough to be able to afford expensive stuff." Kenji frowned, thinking. "Yeah, I'm positive I overheard him tell Mr. Tanaka about it a couple weeks ago while he was at our place."

Detective Maplethorpe spoke up again. "What's this about the war, Kenji?"

Kenji filled him in on his grandfather's wartime years in the internment camp and the deaths of his grandpa's mom and sister, and how Franklin Omura had met Hideki Tanaka there.

"After the war, my great-grandpa moved back to L.A. with Grandpa but couldn't find any work," said Kenji. "He was an architect before getting tossed in the camp, and his old company didn't want him back. Seems nobody was hiring Japanese people on the West Coast then."

I shook my head in disgust. "Haters gonna hate."

"Yeah," said Kenji. "Mr. Tanaka's family moved to L.A., too. They had more luck. His dad actually found a good job. I don't know what it was, Grandpa didn't tell me. After a while, my great-grandpa took my grandpa and they moved to Detroit, where the auto plants were hiring anyone who wanted a job, Japanese or not.

"Grandpa was around seventeen by then," Kenji continued. "His dad found work on one of the Ford assembly lines, and Grandpa enrolled at Wayne State. Ended up graduating summa cum laude. A few years later he met my grandma and they got married. Settled down in Detroit, had my dad in 1960. Grandma died pretty young, my dad was only ten. So Grandpa raised my dad by himself."

"Tell me more about this Tanaka," said Detective Maplethorpe. "When did he come back into the picture?"

"I was just getting to that part. Mr. Tanaka showed up in Detroit around 1975 or so. He found Grandpa and they had a big reunion. They got to be friends again. In 1980, they started sort of a club for internment camp survivors in southeast Michigan. There were more than you'd think around here. Their club had fifty members by the mid-eighties.

"Anyway, eventually the club folded because the members were getting old and kicking the bucket. But Grandpa and Mr. Tanaka have stayed friends ever since. I think they might be the only two camp survivors left around here. He comes by every few weeks. He and Grandpa get pretty blitzed sometimes. It's kind of funny. Grandpa loves to talk, you know? Imagine him with a six pack in him. He'll talk until your ears fall off. And Mr. Tanaka always likes to listen."

"So Tanaka knows about the necklace," said X, almost to himself. "'Cause your gramps told him about it."

"Wait a minute, X," said Kenji. "What're you saying, man? You're not thinking Mr. Tanaka—"

Yusuf broke in. "There was a burglary by someone who probably knew where the safe was and knew there was something valuable inside. And Mr. Tanaka's the only one we know of who matches this description. Plus, as a locksmith, he might know how to crack a safe. Especially one sold by his own business."

"Does this Tanaka need money, Kenji?" asked Detective Maplethorpe. "He in debt, about to lose his house, anything like that?"

"I don't know," Kenji replied. "I don't know anything about his money situation. Maybe Grandpa does."

6

"The cops already talked to me, you guys. They wanted to know about Hideki. John and Jillian told them about how he sold us the safe. So of course they think he did it."

It was evening, and we were all back at Kenji's. Franklin Omura was still wearing his Mork from Ork suspenders and baggy corduroys. He'd switched from last night's red and green checked shirt to a plain T-shirt so white it practically glowed. He was sitting on the old sofa in the man cave where I'd met Mr. Tanaka. A Lions game was playing on the big-screen TV with the sound off.

Honey, the Omuras' golden retriever, sat comfortably on the floor next to the sofa, and Franklin was absentmindedly stroking the dog's ears. She was off in doggie heaven, blissfully unaware of her master's troubles.

"Wait," I said. "How do you know they think he's the one who broke in? They haven't even talked to him yet, have they?"

Franklin shook his head and scratched Honey's ears. Her big tail thumped the floor. "Nope, not yet. But I bet they will soon."

"Mr. O, chill," said X. "They just wanna talk to the guy. It's not like they're gonna drag him away in handcuffs."

Franklin didn't seem to hear him. "There's no way Hideki would break into this house. No way." He kept shaking his head. Honey glanced up at him with her big, sad eyes, as if in sympathy.

"Would this Tanaka cat have any motive for taking the jewelry?" asked X. "I mean, never mind that he's your buddy and everything for a second. Does he even have a motive for doing it in the first place? Like, is he hurting for cash?"

Franklin sighed. "He's not doing so good, fellas. He got divorced a while back. His ex had a good lawyer. She got the car, most of their savings. Almost got the house, too, but Hideki managed to hang onto it. Barely." He lowered his voice to a whisper. "He's on food stamps, you guys. Barely making ends meet. I was really surprised when he cut John and Jillian such a deal on the safe. He can't afford to be giving out big discounts these days."

"So, he needs money," said X. He turned to Kenji. "Can we go peep the crime scene?"

"I guess so," said Kenji. "Come on."

We left Franklin with Honey in the man cave and trooped out to the family room to look at the sliding glass door where the burglar had entered.

"This was unlocked?" asked X.

Kenji nodded. "Yeah. That's what my mom said. But Dad wasn't so sure. He says he remembered locking it that night. But it was unlocked the morning after."

X knelt down and peered at the door's locking mechanism. He slid the door open on its track a few inches and looked at the faceplate and hooks embedded in the edge of the door. He jiggled the handle, watching the hooks move up and down. Then he stood up and draped a long arm around Kenji's shoulder.

"I hate to tell you this, man, but maybe your folks should think about a lock upgrade. This one is pretty low end. Not too hard to pick."

Kenji ducked out from under X's arm. "Okay, yeah, I'll be sure to tell them. Are you saying maybe it was locked, after all?"

"I'm sayin' it's definitely possible. Anyone with a halfway decent set of picks and a little experience could get this open."

X didn't have to say it, but I knew we were all thinking it: someone like a locksmith.

"Let's go check out the safe," said X.

Kenji led us upstairs to his parents' bedroom. The safe sat where we had last seen it, but this time the door was hanging open and the safe was empty.

X got down on his hands and knees while the rest of us stood and watched. He checked out the inside, then he swung the door closed. He moved the handle up and down a few times and took a look at the three heavy steel deadbolts sticking out of the side of the door. There were matching holes on the door frame for the deadbolts to slide into when the safe was locked.

"So Mr. Tanaka really pushed this one on your folks?" asked X. "Gave them a big discount and everything?"

"Yeah, he sweetened the deal for them," Kenji replied. "Nice guy."

"Sweetened the deal," said X, almost to himself. He went silent, and we all knew not to disturb him. We could practically see the gears turning under his big Afro. He was staring down at the carpet in front of the safe.

Then, suddenly, X grabbed the front of the safe and tipped it forward. He laid it on its door, exposing the back.

"What's up, X?" I said.

"What's up?" he repeated, running his fingers around the edge of the rear panel. "What's up is, I'll lay you ten-to-one odds that Mr. Tanaka's the one who robbed this safe."

Kenji looked stunned. "Hang on, X, how do you know that? You said yourself anyone messing with the keypad would've woken up Mom and Dad. How could he have cracked this thing?"

X's fingers had stopped roaming around and were feeling at something under the bottom edge of the back panel. "I didn't say he cracked it. I said he robbed it."

"How?" said Yusuf.

At that moment, X said, "Got it!" and we heard a faint click.

A small, rectangular section of the back panel flipped up, revealing the inside of the empty safe.

X sat back on the floor and pointed at the hidden door. "That's how, my brothers."

7

"How did you—" started Kenji, then snapped his mouth closed.

"How'd I know there was a secret door?" said X. "'Cause I knew whoever did this didn't hack the lock. Too noisy, remember? But they got in somehow. So there had to be another way besides the regular door."

Kenji nodded, looking morose. "I guess I know why Mr. Tanaka wanted my mom and dad to get this safe," he said. "He had it all fitted out, didn't he? I guess that means he knew what they were gonna put in it. Man, this is all so... lame. He's Grandpa's best friend! Grandpa's gonna be... I don't know what. Pretty pissed off."

"Sorry, Kenji," said Yusuf. We all echoed his sentiment.

Something occurred to me. "If Mr. Tanaka's been friends with your grandpa all these years, why would he suddenly decide to rip him off? And he wasn't even ripping off your grandpa, really. He stole from your mom and dad. Why now?"

Kenji shrugged. "I don't know. Maybe he's more hard up for money than Grandpa thinks. Maybe he's jealous. Who knows?"

"Brothers, don't forget there was something else stolen besides the necklace," said X. "Kenji, can we talk to your grandpa about that book?"

"I guess we can try," said Kenji.

We went back upstairs and found Franklin still in the man cave. He was sitting on the couch, his head hung down to his chest, which was hitching with sobs. Honey sat next to him, drowsing. There were several empty cans of Pabst Blue Ribbon on the floor.

"My book..." he mumbled. "Mother, I'm sorry I've let you down... Mother, please forgive me..."

"Grandpa?" said Kenji, putting his hand on the old man's shoulder. "Hey, Grandpa? Can we talk to you? Can we talk to you about that book?"

Franklin turned his tear-streaked face toward Kenji, then looked at the rest of us.

"Sit down, you guys. It's time you heard about Manzanar."

8

"It was me, my mom and dad, and my little sister Ruth," began Franklin, in a subdued voice I'd never heard from him before. "I was twelve and Ruth was six. They put us in a huge camp way out in the California desert. The name of it was Manzanar.

"We arrived there in June of 1942. What I remember most about it was how hot it was. One day, about a week after we got there, it hit a hundred degrees. And the wind. My God, the wind never stopped. Ever. Everything in our little hut got covered with dust, and no matter how many times we swept it off, it would be back an hour later. Sometimes I think all I ever did in that place was sweep. Our hut was a little tarpaper job with an aluminum roof. It kept the wind off us, but it was full of little gaps. That's how the dust would get in, and the cold.

"Anyway, we settled in and tried to make the best of it. My parents were from Japan and they had the real old-school Japanese outlook. Stoic. Tough. They could deal with anything life threw at them. So they made sure my sister and me were as comfortable as possible, without ever thinking about themselves.

"Pretty soon, mom was teaching us our lessons, as much as she could, anyway, so we wouldn't fall behind in school. We all knew we'd be there for the duration of the war, but my folks were real fanatics when it came to education. My dad even managed to get his hands on some old textbooks. I don't know how, but they appeared one day in our hut. We treated them like sacred relics.

"That first summer I remember mostly sweating, learning, and trying to stay out of the windstorms that would come in out of the desert. I made a few friends, too."

"Like Mr. Tanaka?" asked Kenji.

"Yeah, like Hideki. He was about my age and we got to be buddies. We even started a camp baseball team in August. Not too many kids played, though, because of the heat. Hideki was a real mischief-maker back in those days. Always pushing the rules to see what he could get away with. Maybe that's why I liked him. He was a survivor and he fought against all the stupid rules we had to follow. And once he decided he wanted something, he never gave up. Tenacious. That was Hideki. I admired that about him, too.

"So the summer ended and things cooled down, which was a relief. In November, we celebrated a little Thanksgiving with Hideki's family. The camp administration distributed small turkeys to everyone. They turned out to be pretty crappy, but at least it wasn't the usual camp food, which wasn't all that bad but it was the same stuff day in and day out. It got cold in the desert in November, and I caught myself thinking back to the summer heat and wishing we could have some of it back.

"But in December, something happened that made me forget about how cold it was. There was a huge riot. It was early in the month. People fighting all over the camp. I didn't understand what it was about, and my parents didn't really understand, either.

"Later on, after the war, I found out it was because of rumors that the camp administrators were selling some of the food meant for inmates on the black market. That was part of it, anyway. Whatever the cause, the riot went on for two days. The military police were called in and there was some shooting."

At this point, Franklin stopped and closed his eyes. He took a few deep breaths. We all waited patiently for the old man to speak again. I was on the edge of my seat. and it looked like the other guys were, too.

At last, he continued. His voice was even softer now. "It was during this riot that my little sister, Ruth, was killed. For some reason — I never knew why — she had wandered into the part of the camp where the soldiers were shooting. But it wasn't a bullet that did it. It was a rock. A rock thrown by another inmate. It hit her in the temple. She got a concussion from it and fainted. She never woke up."

Tears were streaming down Franklin's face, which looked older than I'd ever seen it. And really tired.

Kenji took his grandpa's hand and squeezed it. "You never told me how she died, Grandpa," Kenji said. "That's horrible."

Franklin nodded. "Yeah. I've missed her every day since. We were really close. But there's more. A photograph was taken of my sister right before the rock was thrown. The picture also showed the person who was about to throw it."

"For real?" said X. "How'd someone get a picture of that? And how'd you know about it?"

"The person who took the photo was another friend of mine in the camp, a kid named Freddie Takeda. He used to carry this big camera around. Photography was his hobby. He happened to be there and saw my sister and took a picture of her. He didn't see the rock-thrower and didn't mean to get him in the frame.

"After Ruth died, Freddie developed the film in a little darkroom he'd set up in an empty hut. How he kept dust out of that place I'll never know, but he did. When he developed the picture, there the guy was in the background. Big rock in his hand, arm cocked back, about to chuck it. And my sister in the foreground, looking scared and lost."

"Freddie took her picture instead of helping her?" asked Yusuf in disbelief.

"Yeah. I never forgave him for that. He died a year or so later from a burst appendix. I'm ashamed to say it now, but I was glad when he died."

"I would've felt the same," said Kenji. "The dude was snapping away when he could've saved her."

"Anger eats you up inside, Kenji," said Franklin. "I found that out. Long after the war ended, I forgave Freddie, and I've been a happier man for it."

"What happened to the picture?" asked X.

"Freddie gave it to me. I think it was his way of trying to make up for not trying to help Ruth. He thought I'd want it to remember her by, and also he thought maybe I could find the guy who threw the rock since he was in the picture, too. But I never did. I searched the camp for six months and never found him."

"Where does the book come in?" asked Kenji.

"The book was all pictures. It was a little scrapbook I made with pictures from Manzanar. I put Freddie's picture of my sister on the last page. I didn't want to, but my mom made me. She wanted to make sure the last picture of my sister got preserved. To honor her memory. She made me promise to keep the book and the picture safe for as long as I lived. I did. I made her that promise. And when she was dying, I made it again."

"Wait, jump back," said X. "Your mom died in that place?"

Kenji shot a warning look at X, but the question was already out. It didn't seem to matter, though. Franklin was well into his six pack and the words were pouring out of him.

"In May 1943. Food poisoning. I never knew what she ate that did it, but she was already weak from the lousy climate and all the dust. She lasted five days before she passed away. She was such a strong woman, my mom was." Franklin smiled a little at the memory. "Yeah. Tough as nails in her own quiet, Japanese way. Anyway, she was lying on her cot in our hut, so sick and weak she couldn't stand up anymore, and she made me promise to keep that book safe. It was her last wish. She died an hour later."

We were all quiet. Honey snored and her paws twitched.

"So that's it," Franklin said sadly. "Now the book is gone, and I've let my mother down. I kept it for seventy-four years, and now it's gone."

9

We were silent for a minute, absorbing what Franklin had told us. I felt like we'd been transported back to the war ourselves, and suddenly any problems I had seemed like chump change compared to what this old man in front of me had experienced.

He looked different to me now, in a way I couldn't put my finger on. He looked... deeper, somehow, like he wasn't just Kenji's funny old grandpa anymore. He had a history I could barely imagine.

"Mr. O," said X. "Did Mr. Tanaka know this book was in the safe?"

Franklin nodded. "Yeah, I mentioned it to him before John and Jillian even bought the safe. I said I was going to keep my Manzanar scrapbook in there, in case there was ever a fire or something."

"Is there any reason why he would've wanted the book?"

"No, not at all... What's this about, X? You're not thinking Hideki did this, are you?"

Kenji spoke up. His voice was gentle. "Grandpa, there's something you oughta see."

He came upstairs with us, and X showed him the secret door in the back of the safe. Franklin just stared at it for what seemed like an eternity. Then he sat down heavily on the edge of the king-sized bed.

"Oh my God," he said. "Why... I don't understand this. Did Hideki put that door in? Why would he do that? I know he's on hard times, but he's my buddy. He knows he can come to me for help!"

Honey, who had followed us upstairs and was sitting next to the bed, licked Franklin's hand and put her head in his lap. He scratched her behind one ear.

"We're sorry, Mr. Omura," said Yusuf. "We know he's your friend. But we don't know how else all of this can be explained. A safe with a secret door sold by Mr. Tanaka to Kenji's parents, a burglar who went to the safe and nowhere else in the house... Whoever it was knew where the safe would be and knew there was something valuable in it. There's no one else who knew all of this except Mr. Tanaka."

Franklin sat silently for a minute, still scratching Honey's head. Her tail thumped softly against the carpet. "That's why you didn't bark, isn't it, girl?" he said softly to the dog. "You knew him. He wasn't a stranger."

"What do you mean, Grandpa?" asked Kenji. "Honey didn't make any noise because she was in the basement that night, like always."

Franklin shook his head ruefully. "Nope. For a couple weeks now, I've been letting her up to sleep in the living room." He glanced at Kenji. "Don't tell your parents, they'll be pissed. But I can't stand her being down there all by herself. I let her sleep on the couch as long as she doesn't go upstairs and bother anyone."

Kenji looked stunned. So did the rest of us, me included. "But that means Honey was right there when the burglar came through the sliding door from outside! And if she didn't bark, that means—"

"That she knew the person," X finished. "Yeah. Mr. O, sorry to say it, but this is all pointing in the same direction. I think Mr. T stole your book and Mrs. O's necklace. But why? That's what I don't understand." He paused and frowned. "Yet."

"I've learned a lot about people during my life," Franklin said. "One thing I've learned is that you can never really know another person's heart, not really. Not the deepest stuff. I can't pretend that all of this doesn't mean what you guys think it means. Hideki is my friend, but I can't deny what I'm seeing." He paused, thinking. "X, maybe we should tell your dad about this and get the police involved."

"Sure can, Mr. O," said X. "But I have a feeling he'll tell me there isn't enough evidence to charge Mr. T with anything. A secret door in the safe and a dog that didn't bark isn't enough. The cops didn't get any fingerprints or anything like that to tie him to the break-in. It's all circumstantial."

Franklin sighed. "Yeah, I see your point, X."

"Sorry, Mr. O."

"There's something else we can do. I'm supposed to go over to his place tomorrow night to play cards. I'll tell him I'm bringing you guys, too. Bring your instruments like you're going to jam, he likes your music. We can confront him with what we know. I'll tell him it's his one chance to come clean with me, his one chance to be honest. If I know Hideki, he's feeling pretty guilty about what he did. I'll ask him to tell me why he did it, and if he still has the necklace."

"And your book," said Yusuf.

"There's no reason why he'd want that thing. He probably chucked it once he saw what it was. But maybe I'll get lucky and he'll still have that and the necklace."

10

The next night, Thursday, we all met at Kenji's place. Franklin had gotten Mr. Tanaka to agree to have the four of us over, too. So we all piled into Kenji's grandpa's old Mercury station wagon and drove to Livonia, just west of Redford, where Mr. Tanaka lived. We pulled up outside a modest two-story blue bungalow with a neat little flower garden out front.

We grabbed our instrument cases and amps (except Yusuf, since Mr. Tanaka said he had an old drum kit that had belonged to one of his kids back in the day) and went up to the front door. A little wooden sign read "Welcome" in fancy engraved script.

Franklin rang the bell. Mr. Tanaka answered a minute later, wearing jeans and an old Tigers jersey and holding a Budweiser. He grinned when he saw us.

"Hey, everyone, come on in!" He swept his arm aside, gesturing for us to enter.

As we did, he gave a little bow from the waist. Franklin chuckled and bowed back. "Gotta keep those old-country traditions alive, right, Frankie?" Mr. Tanaka said.

"You've never even been to Japan, old man," said Franklin. "But whatever you say."

"Yeah, okay, you caught me." Mr. Tanaka tipped us a wink as he said this. "Never even been as far as Hawaii, to tell the truth."

We all walked into a small living room furnished with what looked like half of an IKEA catalog. There was some ugly, store-bought artwork on the walls. A small fireplace was built into one wall.

As I followed Mr. Tanaka and the others through the room, I detected an odd smell. It was too faint for me to be able to identify it. For some reason, it reminded me of going camping. I didn't give it any thought. Not at the time, anyway.

"Come on downstairs," said Mr. Tanaka.

We followed him through a small but neat kitchen and down a set of wooden stairs into a large room. The drum kit sat in a far corner. We began to set up while the two men went through an open door to one side and into a smaller room that contained a wet bar. A card table and two chairs were set up in the middle of the room.

"You boys play as long as you want," said Mr. Tanaka. "It'll be good to have some background music. Maybe it'll distract this card shark here so I can actually win a few hands." He pointed at Franklin, who laughed.

"Right on, Mr. T," said X. "And thanks."

Mr. Tanaka gave a thumbs-up and closed the door. I unpacked my Fender Strat and fiddled with the tuning keys. Yusuf had already planted himself behind the kit, which was a beat-up old Ludwig, and was trying out a few quick drum fills on it. Kenji unzipped his gig bag and took out his Fender bass.

"You fellas notice that smell up there in Mr. T's living room?" asked X, one long arm draped over a mic stand he'd just set up.

"Yeah," I said. "It smelled familiar for some reason. Reminded me of going camping with my mom and dad when I was little. But I couldn't place it. I figured it was just the fireplace. Probably reminded me of campfires or something."

"It was coming from the fireplace for sure," said X. "But it wasn't burned wood. It was burned plastic. Ain't no other smell like it. It was pretty faint, though. Been a while since it was fresh."

I snapped my fingers. "Now I remember. On this one camping trip up north, Houghton Lake, when I was about six, my dad accidentally dropped his glasses into the campfire one night. The frames were plastic. They melted. Stank like crazy. Mom was really pissed. That's why the smell reminded me of camping."

"Right on," said X. "Hang tight, dudes. Make some noise. I'm gonna bounce back upstairs for a minute."

Before any of us could say anything, X was gone, bounding like a gazelle, Afro waving around his head like a great big ball of dark-colored cotton candy.

Per X's instructions, we proceeded to make some noise. We messed around with "Play That Funky Music," giving me a chance to run through the guitar solo a couple of times. It wasn't as smooth as I wanted it to be, but it was getting there.

X came back down about five minutes later. He was holding something in one hand, a small, charred scrap of paper. It was orange.

"Brothers, I found this in Mr. T's fireplace." X's voice was heavy. "I was kinda hoping I wouldn't, but… yeah, anyway, have a look." He held out the paper flat on his palm.

It turned out not to be paper at all, but plastic. A small piece of orange plastic, about the size of a quarter, charred and melted around the edges.

"Grandpa's book," Kenji whispered. "It was bound with—"

"Orange plastic," I finished. "Yeah, I saw it when your mom showed us the necklace."

"This is all I found," said X. "I dug around in the ashes in that fireplace until I thought I was gonna choke. Dude needs to clean that thing out."

"Maybe Mr. Tanaka burned something else made of orange plastic," said Yusuf. "It could be a coincidence, right?"

"Yeah," said X. "It could be. Except for one thing." He turned the piece of plastic over. On the other side, stamped into the plastic in small block capitals, were the letters F.G.O.

We all looked at Kenji.

"Grandpa's middle name is George," Kenji said. "Franklin George Omura. In case you're wondering."

11

At that moment, we heard Franklin Omura's voice from the next room. He was speaking loudly.

"Why do you deny it, Hideki? Why do you insult me like this? We're friends! Or so I thought."

"I'm telling you, Frankie, I didn't bust into your place, and I didn't steal anything!" Mr. Tanaka was nearly yelling.

"Then how do you explain a secret opening in the safe that you sold to my son and daughter-in-law? Just a damned coincidence?" Franklin shouted the last word. "Have you no shame, Hideki? Have you no integrity?"

Just then X walked over to the door leading to the smaller room, and before any of us could stop him, he opened it.

"Hey, Mr. O, Mr. T! Chill out, dudes. I got something to show you."

Yusuf, Kenji, and I gathered at the doorway. X stood at the table, his six-foot, stork-like frame towering over the two men seated there. Franklin was scowling at Mr. Tanaka, who looked shocked. They both turned and stared at X.

"X, what's going on here?" said Mr. Tanaka. "This is private business between two adults."

"I know, I know," said X. "Sorry. This'll just take a sec." He dropped the piece of plastic onto the table. It landed with Franklin's initials face-up. "I found this in your fireplace, Mr. T."

Both men stared at the piece of plastic for a moment, then Mr. Tanaka jumped to his feet. Standing, he beat X's height by a good three inches.

"What?" he said. "My fireplace? What were you doing in my fireplace, X?" He looked furious, and he stalked over to the wet bar and put his hands down flat on it as if to anchor himself. "Why were you snooping around my house?"

He actually said snooping, I thought. *Don't people only say that in bad detective stories?*

Franklin was inspecting the plastic. He looked up at Mr. Tanaka. "Hideki, this looks like it came from the cover of my Manzanar scrapbook. These are even my initials here. How can you explain this? Why was this in your fireplace?"

As I watched from the doorway, everyone seemed to freeze in place. X, standing on one side of the card table, his long arms folded; Franklin, still seated and holding the piece of plastic out towards Mr. Tanaka; and Mr. Tanaka himself, standing and staring, dumbstruck, at

Franklin. Mr. Tanaka's face was a mask of anger and confusion.

Then, slowly, Mr. Tanaka held out his hand. Franklin placed the plastic into his friend's open palm. Mr. Tanaka raised it to his face and stared closely, as if trying to see into it. Then he closed his eyes for a long moment. When he opened them again, they were wet, and his angry expression was gone. His lips trembled as he spoke.

"Frankie, Frankie, what have I done...?" he whispered, and sank down into his chair. The bit of orange plastic dropped from his hand onto the table. "Oh, my God, what have I done?"

Franklin stared hard across the table at Mr. Tanaka. "Why, Hideki? Why did you do it? Was it the necklace? Do you need money? Why didn't you just ask me? I would have helped you out, don't you know that? We've known each other for so long, surely you know I'd help my oldest friend."

But Mr. Tanaka was shaking his head in sorrow. "No, no, it wasn't the necklace," he said quietly. "I wanted your book, Frankie. Your scrapbook of Manzanar."

"My book... What? Why the hell would you want that thing? Just a bunch of old pictures of a place you and I both remember too well already?"

"There was a certain picture in it. It... it caused me such shame when you showed it to me." Mr. Tanaka put his hands over his face and wept.

"But... which one?" said Franklin.

His voice muffled by his hands and choked with tears, Mr. Tanaka replied, "The one of your little sister. The one Freddie Takeda took. The one with the guy in the background about to throw the rock."

Mr. Tanaka couldn't speak for what seemed like a long time. Then he raised his tear-stained face to Franklin's. "The guy with the rock was my father. My father killed your little sister."

12

The small room was utterly silent. The only sound I could hear was a very low buzz from one of our amps out in the rec room.

Finally, Franklin broke the silence. His voice seemed jarringly loud. "That was your father, Hideki?" He sounded confused. "But... are you sure?"

"I know my own father's face, Frankie. Wouldn't you recognize yours if you saw it in a photo? Even one that's seventy years old? It was him. He would have been in his early forties during the riot. I remember he came back to our hut after it was over and he looked scared. Really scared. I just assumed it was because of all the violence he saw. But when I saw your picture, I remembered he was drunk that day. Dad was always a mean drunk. Really nice guy sober but he'd pick fights for no reason when he was on the sauce. Booze eventually killed him, in the fifties.

"But, yeah, I saw him in the picture with that rock in his hand, and I remembered he'd gotten his hands on some black market whiskey somewhere, and he'd gone to see the riot while he was still blitzed. I'd forgotten all about that."

"He might've gotten mean, but mean enough to kill a little girl?" said Franklin.

Mr. Tanaka nodded sadly. "Dad didn't know what the hell he was doing half the time when he was drunk, Frankie. One time, he threw me down the stairs. I was about five years old. He always claimed it was an accident, but Mom knew better and told me so after he died. He was like Jekyll and Hyde, sober and drunk."

"You broke into my family's home and stole from them, Hideki. And for what? To cover up evidence of something your drunkard father did decades ago?"

"I'm so sorry, Frankie," said Mr. Tanaka. "I couldn't bear having you figure out what my family had done to yours. Ever since you first showed me that picture, years ago, I've wanted to get it from you somehow. And—"

"And when you found out Mr. and Mrs. O wanted a safe for that necklace, you saw your chance," finished X.

Franklin looked at him, startled, as if he'd forgotten X and the rest of us were there. But Mr. Tanaka just nodded.

"Yes," he said. "Yes. That's what happened."

"What about the necklace, Hideki? Where is it?"

Instead of answering, Mr. Tanaka went over behind the wet bar and bent over. He fished something out from underneath it and stood up. Draped over his fingers was the necklace I remembered seeing the day of our last band practice: a cluster of small diamonds and two larger, deep blue sapphires, all suspended on a fine gold chain.

"I wanted to give it back," he said. "I was waiting for a chance to return it somehow." He looked more ashamed than ever.

"Why'd you even take it if all you really wanted was my book?" said Franklin.

Yusuf answered before anyone else could. "I think Mr. Tanaka took the necklace so it would appear to be an ordinary burglary. Right?"

"Yeah," said Franklin. "I see now. You picked the cheap lock on the sliding glass door, went up to the safe, opened the secret door, and grabbed both things so everyone would focus on the necklace and think the book was an afterthought. That about right?"

Mr. Tanaka nodded. "I'm so sorry, Frankie. I have no right to ask this, but do you think you can find it in yourself to forgive me someday, old friend?"

Franklin stood up, drawing himself up to his full height and crossing his arms over his chest. And even though Kenji's grandfather was only about five-foot four and had never been to Japan, suddenly I could see a trace of his proud ancestors in his face and in the way he stood. A samurai sword wouldn't have looked out of place in his hand just then.

"Hideki," Franklin said slowly, "I have already forgiven you. Our friendship came out of the war and the camps and can never be broken. We will always be friends."

At that, Mr. Tanaka put his head into his hands and began sobbing.

"But," Franklin continued, "you will no longer be welcome in my son's home. You are not to come there again. And I can no longer come here, out of respect for him, his wife, and their son, whose home you invaded. We will never see each other again, Hideki. Never."

13

Kenji's parents ended up deciding not to press charges against Mr. Tanaka since they got the necklace back, but they demanded a full refund on the safe. Needless to say, they got it.

None of us ever saw Mr. Tanaka again. A few weeks later, Franklin told us he'd sold his house and moved away somewhere. Franklin didn't know where and said he didn't care.

Franklin's book was toast (literally). That little piece of half-melted plastic was all that was left. Franklin was sad that all of the Manzanar pictures were gone, and especially the one of his little sister, but he stopped blaming himself for it.

And best of all, he saw that he hadn't broken his promise to his mother at all. Keeping the book in that safe was the best thing he could have done, and he'd had no way of knowing what his old friend had been up to.

* * *

A month later we were all over at Kenji's place again for practice, and Franklin came down to watch us play. He was in his usual wacky
outfit: Mork from Ork suspenders, plaid shirt, the whole deal. He did his air guitar and air drum routines, which cracked all of us up. When we'd run through a few songs, he called a time out.

"You guys," he said after taking a swig from his ever-present Pabst Blue Ribbon beer can, "I never thanked you for what you did. For figuring out what happened to my book. So... thanks. I really mean that." He looked at each of us in turn, directly in the eye, and for a moment I saw an echo of his Japanese ancestors in his face, just like in Mr. Tanaka's basement.

"Hideki's pride led him to sacrifice his honor, and that is never a good bargain. Remember that. Honor is more important than pride, every time." He pointed at himself. "Just because I wear these crazy clothes and drink American beer and have never set foot in Japan in my life doesn't mean those old Japanese ideas aren't important to me. Hideki sacrificed his honor. Don't ever sacrifice yours."

We were all silent for a minute, taking this in. Franklin had never made a speech before, and he'd really gotten our attention. The winter wind blew hard outside the house, and I could have sworn I heard a samurai yell mixed in with it. Probably just my imagination.

Then Franklin took another pull from his beer. "All right, enough of this heavy stuff," he said with his biggest, goofiest grin. "Come on, People Movers! Gimme an encore!"

About The Author

Brian Kirchner is 46 years old and teaches Geology at Henry Ford College, near Detroit, Michigan. He lives in Royal Oak, Michigan, with his wife and three kids. Brian has loved writing fiction since a very young age but took a (very) long hiatus from it while earning a doctorate in Geology and starting a family. Since taking up writing again in 2016, Brian has published a short story in the online literary magazine "Inklette," he was awarded 9th place in a Writer's Digest international poetry competition, and he has published a short humor piece at the online site "Funny in Five Hundred." Brian has also written a novel and is currently shopping it around to literary agencies.

Besides writing and teaching about rocks, Brian enjoys playing guitar and banjo, reading (just about anything), road trips, astronomy, and pizza.

About The Publisher

Story Shares is a nonprofit focused on supporting the millions of teens and adults who struggle with reading by creating a new shelf in the library specifically for them. The ever-growing collection features content that is compelling and culturally relevant for teens and adults, yet still readable at a range of lower reading levels.

Story Shares generates content by engaging deeply with writers, bringing together a community to create this new kind of book. With more intriguing and approachable stories to choose from, the teens and adults who have fallen behind are improving their skills and beginning to discover the joy of reading. For more information, visit storyshares.org.

Easy to Read. Hard to Put Down.

Made in the USA
Middletown, DE
21 January 2023

22543321R10057